OUTSIDE, INSIDE

LeUyen Pham

Roaring Brook Press
New York

Published by Roaring Brook Press
Roaring Brook Press is a division of
Holtzbrinck Publishing Holdings Limited Partnership
120 Broadway, New York, NY 10271 • mackids.com

ISBN 978-1-250-79835-0
Library of Congress Control Number 2020910781

Our books may be purchased in bulk for promotional, educational,
or business use. Please contact your local bookseller or the Macmillan
Corporate and Premium Sales Department at (800) 221-7945 ext. 5442
or by email at MacmillanSpecialMarkets@macmillan.com.

First edition, 2021 • Book design by Sharismar Rodriguez
The illustrations for this book were born digital.
Printed in China by Hung Hing Off-Set Printing Co. Ltd., Heshan City, Guangdong Province

10 9 8 7 6 5 4

Something strange happened on an unremarkable day just before the season changed.

Everybody who was

OUTSIDE...

. . . went INSIDE.

Everyone.

Everywhere.

All
over
the
WORLD.

Everyone just went inside,
shut their doors,

and WAITED.

Some people

NEEDED to be . . .

. . . where they
NEEDED to be.

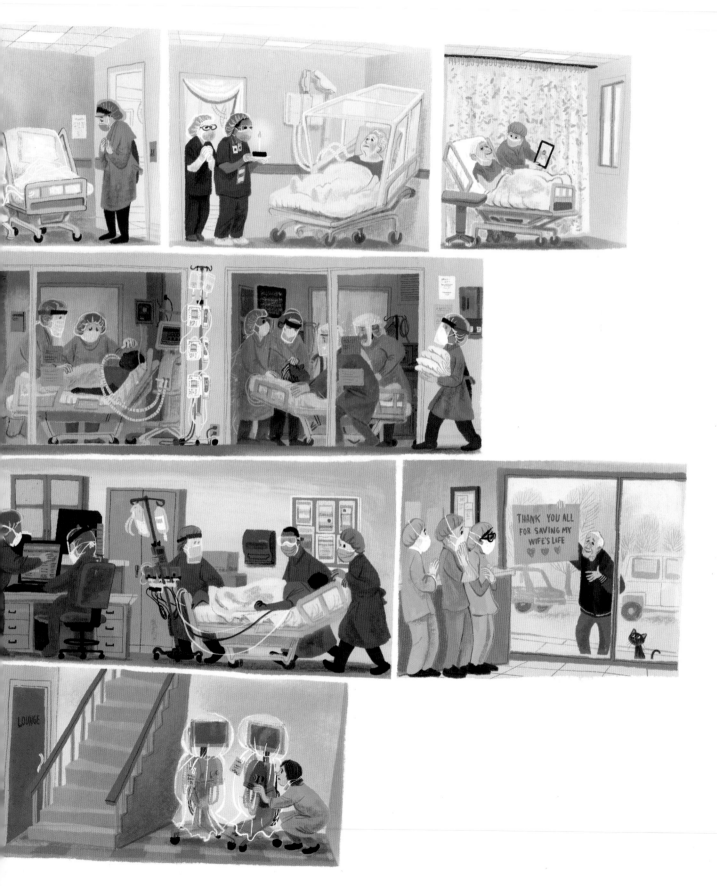

OUTSIDE,
the sky was quiet,

but the wind still blew

and
birds
kept
singing.

Raccoons
came out

and squirrels
played in
the streets,

but the cars stayed away.

The world felt
a little different.

INSIDE,
we baked
and
cooked,

made
music
and watched TV.

We read
and played
games.

Some of us worked a little,
some of us worked a lot . . .

and some of us
couldn't work
at all.

We all felt
a little different.

OUTSIDE,
there were fences
both real
and pretend.

Swings sat still,
and slides
were lonely.

Bells didn't ring,
and halls
were empty.

We had birthdays
without parties,

shared words
without sounds,

and
reached
each other
without
touching.

The world was changing
a tiny bit outside.

INSIDE,
we waited

and we worried,

we
laughed

and we cried,

and we tried to breathe.

We made things
together

and did
things
alone.

We hoped
and prayed
and wished.

We were all changing
a tiny bit inside.

OUTSIDE,
the
world
kept
growing.

INSIDE,

we kept growing too.

So why did we
all go inside?

Well . . .

... there were
lots of reasons.

But mostly
because
everyone
knew

it was the right
thing to do.

On the OUTSIDE,
we are all different.

But on the INSIDE,

And we remembered
that soon

spring would come.

. . . and

OUTSIDE.

INSIDE...

AUTHOR'S NOTE

The winter of 2019 seemed much like any other. There were holidays and family gatherings, school projects due, and work deadlines. People took trains and buses to work, and planes zigzagged across the skies. We were out and about—talking, eating, and living as we always had. Until something changed. A virus had entered the world, gradually making its way from city to city, country to country, continent to continent.

Almost overnight, everything that had once seemed normal was no longer so, as one by one, to prevent spreading the virus, nearly everyone, everywhere, went inside and closed their doors.

It was difficult to process how quickly things changed. There was a sense, suddenly, that wherever we were in the world, we were cut off. Everyone stayed home, and neighbors next door felt millions of miles apart. The streets and skies seemed eerily quiet and impossibly empty. The world outside felt different.

Inside, we felt different too. People with immunity disorders, health issues, and the elderly (including my own mother undergoing chemotherapy and my father at his nursing home) were in great danger. We worried about getting sick, or getting our loved ones sick. Some of us couldn't work. Some of us couldn't go to school, even online. Some of us couldn't be there for our families when they needed us. Many businesses closed, some temporarily and some permanently. We had no idea what was going to happen next. It was as if the whole world was holding its breath, waiting.

But not everyone stayed inside. Doctors and nurses, the first responders to this pandemic, were on the front lines. With few resources and even less preparation, these incredible heroes rose to the challenge and threw themselves into battling the virus, often putting their own lives at risk. Grocery store employees, delivery people, city workers, and other essential workers compromised their own safety to keep our world running. There were long lines at food banks serving struggling families hard-hit by the lockdown.

In those first weeks of quarantine, I started sketching moments from each day. It was my way of coping with events as they unfolded. On walks around our neighborhood, I began to notice small things. Neighbors smiled beneath masks and greeted each other on the street. Teddy bears began appearing in windows for children to hunt for. Paper hearts decorated doors and fences. Sidewalks were vibrant with chalk drawings of rainbows, and signs on lawns read "We Are In This Together" and "We Can Do This." Neighbors shopped for those unable to and left groceries on doorsteps. Every evening at the same hour, people stepped onto porches or stoops and cheered for those on the front lines, a moment of the day when we were all united in love. Around the world, empty parks saw a resurgence

of wildlife as animals ventured out, undisturbed by humans. Without planes and cars, the air seemed cleaner.

During this difficult time, people reached across the void to find one another and come together. So much had changed, but those struggles, rather than bringing us down, instead brought out the best in many of us. As I write these words, masked people of every color fill the streets to fight against racism and to right the injustices of the world. They face the double danger of contracting the virus and having violence brought against them for speaking their minds.

Nearly every face painted in this book is inspired by a real person, from people in the news to family, friends, and neighbors. The images inside the hospital are based on real events: a woman giving birth while suffering from the virus; an older woman, isolated from her family, celebrating her birthday with kindly nurses the day before she died; the grateful man showing through the hospital window his love for the nurses who saved his wife's life. Stories that moved me found their way into my drawings. One of the most difficult spreads for me to create was the one explaining why we sacrificed as we did. It features real people who were in most danger during this time—some who have either survived or succumbed to the virus—and includes friends who have lost loved ones. Knowing that every character is based on someone real gives me both joy and pain.

My career has been devoted to drawing the world as I would like it to be, my version of a happy world. This is the first time that I have cataloged the world as it is. It is a recording of the daily acts of kindness and humanity made by everyday people. And there was so much happening, so many good deeds, that I simply couldn't find space in these pages to record it all. This book is a time capsule of our moment in history, when the world came together as one to do the right thing.

Uyen Pham JUNE 2020

This book is humbly and gratefully dedicated to those first responders and essential workers whose sacrifices and dedication to life is immeasurable. The world is in your debt.